The Musicians
of Bremen

Other brilliant stories to collect:

The
Musicians of
Bremen

Retold by
Ann Jungman

Illustrated by
James Marsh

■**SCHOLASTIC**
Home of the Story

Scholastic Children's Books,
Commonwealth House, 1–19 New Oxford Street,
London WC1A 1NU, UK
a division of Scholastic Ltd
London ~ New York ~ Toronto ~ Sydney ~ Auckland
Mexico City ~ New Delhi ~ Hong Kong

First published by Scholastic Ltd, 2001

ISBN 0 439 99757 7

Printed by Cox and Wyman Ltd, Reading, Berks.

2 4 6 8 10 9 7 5 3

"Move it there, you brute," shouted the miller at his donkey, and he rained blows on the poor beast's back.

The donkey began to walk forward slowly, weighed down by the two enormous heavy sacks of grain.

"Faster!" yelled the miller, getting

even more angry. "Speed it up there or it's the knacker's yard for you, you ancient useless bag of bones."

The donkey's eyes filled with tears. For years he had served his master well but now he was getting old and the sacks weighed heavy on his back. He tried to go faster but he tripped and fell. Some of the precious golden corn fell on to the road.

"Now look what you've done!" screamed the miller. "You've spilled some of my grain."

At that moment the miller's wife ran out of the front door.

"That donkey is beginning to cost us money, husband. Tomorrow, take him to the knacker's yard. We may make some money out of him when they turn the useless brute into glue."

That night the donkey waited till everyone was in bed and then quietly crept out of his stable and on to the great highway. Trotting along under the stars the donkey felt happy and

free. "After a life of service and hard work I deserve a peaceful old age," he said to himself. "I shall go to the great city of Bremen," he said excitedly. "Yes, and I'll become a street musician. The good people of Bremen will pay me to make my sweet music for them."

As the donkey walked along the empty road he practised his singing: "Ee-aw, ee-aw, ee-aw," he sang happily to himself.

Just then he heard a panting sound. In the light of the moon the donkey could just make out a hunting dog lying exhausted by the roadside.

and became so short he...
...But how the going to...
...bread...

..."But..."Oh," I am...
after you?" cried...thank you for...

...seeing my master too...

"Are you all right?" asked the donkey kindly.

"Not really," replied the dog gloomily. "You see, I am getting old and tired and can no longer run as fast as the other hounds in the hunt."

"Well," agreed the donkey, "that is the way of it; we all get old in the end."

"I know," nodded the dog. "But my master got so angry with me he said

he'd beat me to death, so I've run away. But how I am going to earn my bread I do not know."

"Dear friend, how happy I am to meet you," cried the donkey, "for my situation is somewhat similar. After serving my master, the miller, for many a long year carrying great loads, he wants to send me to the knacker's yard. Like you I have run away to escape my fate."

"How cruel and ungrateful these masters are," sighed the dog and he put his head on his paws and looked miserable.

"Cheer up," said the donkey. "Don't despair, I know just what we should do. I'm on my way to Bremen to become a town musician."

"A town musician?" exclaimed the dog. "What are they?"

"Oh, town musicians, dear dog, are very fortunate folk. They sit in the centre of the city, in the market or by the fountain or some such and play

music. Yes, they make everyone happy and in exchange the people give them money."

"You can buy meat with money," said the dog cheering up and beginning to wag his tail. "Yes, I like the idea of being a musician. What a piece of luck meeting you. Come on, let's set off for Bremen together."

In no time the dog and the donkey were the best of friends. The dog listened spellbound as the donkey told him about the wonderful city of Bremen.

"Oh, I've been there often, very often with my master. You never saw the like. Great cobbled streets and a cathedral that reaches right up into the clouds, grand houses everywhere and a fountain built with water that comes out of the mouths of stone horses. Oh, you'll just love living there."

Then a voice came out of the darkness: "A donkey and a dog, walking along my road in the middle of the

night. Well, well, well, what can be going on, I wonder?"

There by the roadside sat a scrawny, sad-looking cat.

"Our masters don't want us any more because we are old," the donkey told the cat. "So we're off to Bremen to become street musicians."

"Singing in the street for money?" asked the cat.

"Exactly," agreed the donkey and the dog.

"Oh please, please could I come too?" begged the cat. "Cats are famous for their singing and I am known to be particularly musical."

"You'd be very welcome," said the donkey. "A professional musician would be a great asset, but we couldn't take you away from your home."

"They don't want me any more," said the cat sadly. "You see, I am getting a bit old and can't catch mice like I used to. In fact my mistress talks daily of drowning me."

"Never!" cried the donkey. "How ungrateful these people are. My dear cat, you must definitely come with us."

So the three set off into the dark night while at the same time getting to know each other and enjoying the sweet taste of freedom. After a while the golden light of dawn lit up the surrounding country and in the distance they heard the sound of a cock.

"Cock-a-doodle-doo," it shrieked again and again and again.

"I know they're supposed to greet the dawn liked that," complained the dog, "but that cock is just going on and on. I do wish he'd stop."

"It's a horrible racket," agreed the cat. "So different from the sweet sound we cats make when we sing."

As they got closer to the sound they saw that there was a farm and on the gatepost sat the cock screeching away.

"You're giving us all a headache," shouted the donkey. "Why are you yelling like that?"

"My mistress is going to kill me and cook me in the big pot today," wept the cock. "So I am making a big noise while I still have breath to do it, for by tonight I'll be nothing but a stew."

"That is too terrible," cried the donkey. "You must come with us. We're off to be street musicians in Bremen. You've got a terrific voice, you'll help us to get rich."

The cock was very happy with this idea and set off down the road with the other three. They walked all day and as they went they sang the jolly song the donkey had made up for them.

"We're off to Bremen to see the sea,
Musicians we four will always be.
Ee-aw, woof, woof, meow, meow,
  cock-a-doodle-doo.

Each one will give us a whole pound,
We four will make such a golden sound.
Ee-aw, woof, woof, meow, meow,
  cock-a-doodle-doo.

We'll charm the city with our sweet song,
Our stay in Bremen, it will be long.
Ee-aw, woof, woof, meow, meow,
  cock-a-doodle-doo."

In the evening they came to a forest.

"We'll rest here for the night," the donkey told them, "and continue to Bremen tomorrow."

"I'm hungry," complained the dog.

"I'm thirsty," moaned the cat.

"I'm cold," groaned the cock.

"Maybe this Bremen idea wasn't such a grand notion after all," sniffed the dog. "What we need is a roof over

our heads, a fire and some food."

"I'll see what I can do," said the donkey. "I can see a light over there, that might be a place we could shelter. Don't despair at the first hurdle my friends, fame and wealth lie ahead of us."

They approached the lighted house. The donkey went and peeped through the window.

"What can you see?" whispered the cat.

"Robbers," said the donkey. "Surrounded by all their loot, and a big fire and a table groaning with legs of lamb and vegetables and chocolate and the best wine."

"A robbers' house. . . Do you think they'd give us some food if we asked nicely?" questioned the cock.

"Definitely not," replied the donkey. "You know what people are like and robbers are worse than most. We'll have to find a way to get them out. I think I have a little plan."

"Oh, tell," said the dog and the cat and the cock together.

"I'll stand on my hind legs and put my forelegs on the window-sill. You, dog, must climb on to my back and cat, you get on the dog's back."

"And I'll stand at the very top," said the cock proudly.

"Yes, and we'll all sing at once," finished off the donkey.

So the donkey brayed and the dog howled and the cat meowed and the cock crowed, and then they all fell through the window breaking the glass.

The robbers were terrified: "Ghosts!" they shouted. "Let's get out of here. Help!!!" And they took to their heels and ran out of the door into the dark forest as fast as their legs could carry them.

As soon as they managed to stop laughing the four friends sat down at the table and ate every last scrap.

"I'm full and exhausted," announced the dog.

"Me too," sighed the cat.

"I haven't eaten so well for years," said the cock happily. "Cock-a-doodle-doo."

"What a good day this has been," said the donkey contentedly. "Not only are we all alive and free, we are warm and well fed also. Now all we need to end a perfect day is a good rest."

So that's what they did. The animals all had their different ways of sleeping. The cat curled up by the dying fire, the dog lay down by the back door, the donkey went outside into the yard and the cock sat on the fence. And they all slept very deeply indeed. What the animals didn't know was that the robbers were still outside and had seen the lights go out.

"We've got to go back, boys, and get our loot," said the chief robber.

"But Chief, what about the g-g-g-ghost?" asked a robber.

"We scared too easily," said the chief robber. "It was probably some tree falling that alarmed us. Come on, we'll go back in. Nothing to be afraid of, follow me."

So under the cover of darkness the robbers crept towards the cottage and the sleeping animals. One peeped in through the window. "It's very quiet in there," he whispered to the gang. "I'll go in first and look around." And he pushed open the door and went in.

"I can't see a thing in the dark," he said to himself. "I'll just strike a light. There is still one hot gleaming coal in the grate."

But what the robber had seen was not a coal but one gleaming cat's eye. When the match struck against the poor cat's eye, the cat howled in pain

and jumped up and sprang at the robber's face, spitting and scratching.

"Help!" shouted the robber and he tried to stumble out of the back door. He tripped on the dog, who woke up for a moment and bit him hard on the leg. As the robber ran into the donkey, the donkey yawned in his sleep and kicked him hard in the back. The cock was woken up by all the noise and screeched "Kikeriki! Kikeriki! Kikeriki!" and then went back to sleep.

The robber staggered away, bleeding and trembling. Eventually he found the rest of the band.

"Oh Chief, Chief, don't ever go into that house again, there is a terrible witch in there. Look what she did to me. . . Look at the way she scratched me with her long nails. But that wasn't the end of it, my friends, oh no – it got worse, much worse. At the back door there was a man with a knife and he stabbed me in the leg."

"No!" cried the robbers horrified.

"Yes," he insisted, showing them his wounded leg. "And it didn't stop there. In the yard was a hideous monster and he struck me with a club — look at my bruises. Oh, what a night I've had of it."

"You've had a rough time all right," said the chief robber.

"You're right," moaned the robber, "and you haven't heard the end yet. On the fence sat a judge crying, 'Bring the scoundrels to me,' again and again."

"That does it, we'd better get right away from here," decided the chief robber. "We don't want to end up in

jail or hanging from a rope. Best leave the loot and get as far away as possible before something worse happens."

"Yes!" they all shouted. "Let's go and never come back."

The next day the donkey woke his friends up. "Come on, dear friends, we have eaten and drunk to our hearts' content. Now it is time we left for Bremen, we've a living to earn."

"But I would prefer to stay here," said the cat. "It is quiet and safe and there are lots of mice. I would never have to worry about being hungry here. I'm not one bit sure I would like big city living."

"Woof, I like it here too," agreed the dog. "There are hundreds of rabbits for me to chase. And you know, I think I'm a country sort of a dog when all is said and done."

"Plenty of corn for me too," nodded the cock. "And really, you know we can't rely on the kindness of people. Our histories have told us that.

Would you really mind if we stayed here a bit longer, dear noble friend donkey?"

"Well there is plenty of grass for me around here," said the donkey contentedly. "We'll stay on and practise our singing and then go on to Bremen when we feel ready."

"We need lots and lots of practice," said the dog quickly.

"Yes indeed," added the cat. "Years and years of practice."

"Let's practise and go when we all feel it's right," agreed the cock.

And so the four friends stayed in the house very happily and never quite made it to Bremen. But whenever anyone passed near the house they heard this very odd song wafting across the field.

"We're off to Bremen to see the sea,
Musicians we four will always be.
Ee-aw, woof, woof, meow, meow,
  cock-a-doodle-doo.

Each one will give us a whole pound,
We four will make such a golden sound.
Ee-aw, woof, woof, meow, meow,
  cock-a-doodle-doo.

We'll charm the city with our sweet song,
Our stay in Bremen, it will be long.
Ee-aw, woof, woof, meow, meow,
  cock-a-doodle-doo."

Other stories to collect:

The Ugly Duckling

Helen Dunmore

Illustrated by Robin Bell Corfield

Once upon a time there was an ugly duckling
that didn't have a friend in the world…

Orpheus in the
Land of the Dead

Dennis Hamley

Illustrated by Stuart Robertson

Once upon a time there was a musician so fine
that even the dead were charmed…

The Little Mermaid

Linda Newbery

Illustrated by Bee Willey

Once upon a time there was a mermaid
who rescued a prince from drowning…

Beauty and
the Beast

Tessa Krailing

Illustrated by Diana Mayo

Once upon a time there was a beautiful girl
who was forced to live with a hideous Beast…

King Herla's Ride

Jan Mark

Illustrated by Jac Jones

Once upon a time there was a king who lived
upon a hill and a king who lived under one…

The Pedlar of Swaffham

Philippa Pearce

Illustrated by Rosamund Fowler

Once upon a time there was a pedlar
who had an unforgettable dream…

Hansel and Gretel

Henrietta Branford

Illustrated by Lesley Harker

Once upon a time there were a brother and sister
who were left alone in the forest...

Mossycoat

Philip Pullman

Illustrated by Peter Bailey

Once upon a time there was a beautiful girl
whose mother made her a magical, mossy coat...

Aesop's Fables

Malorie Blackman

Illustrated by Patrice Aggs

Once upon a time there was a man named Aesop
who told stories full of wisdom...

The Snow Queen

Berlie Doherty

Illustrated by Sian Bailey

Once upon a time there was a little boy
whose heart was turned to ice...

The Twelve Dancing Princesses

Anne Fine

Illustrated by Debi Gliori

Once upon a time there were twelve princesses,
and no one knew why their shoes were
full of holes…

The Goose Girl

Gillian Cross

Illustrated by Jason Cockcroft

Once upon a time there was a princess
who lost everything she had ever owned…

The Pied Piper

K M Peyton

Illustrated by Victor Ambrus

Once upon a time there was a town
infested with a plague of horrible rats...

The Three Heads
in the Well

Susan Gates

Illustrated by Sue Heap

Once upon a time there were two stepsisters —
one good, one bad — who both went out to seek
their fortunes...